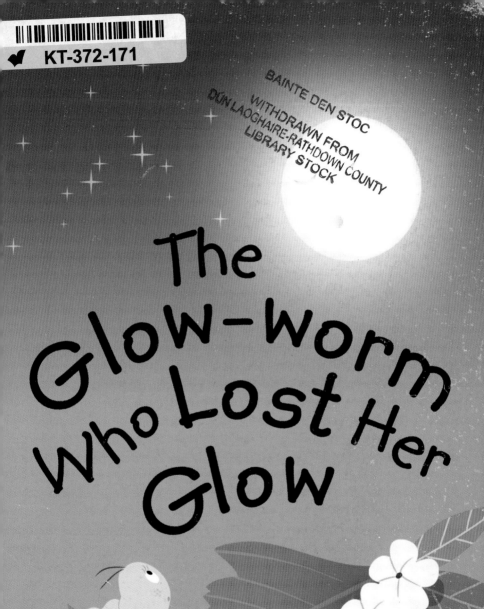

The Glow-worm Who Lost Her Glow

For Rebecca Price
W.B.

S.J.

First published in Great Britain 2004
by Egmont UK Ltd
239 Kensington High Street, London W8 6SA
Text copyright © William Bedford 2004
Illustrations copyright © Sophie Joyce 2004
The author and illustrator have asserted their moral rights.
ISBN 978 1 4052 0976 2
ISBN 1 4052 0976 3
10 9 8 7 6 5 4 3
A CIP catalogue record for this title is available from the British Library.
Printed in Singapore.

The Glow-worm Who Lost Her Glow

By William Bedford

Illustrated by Sophie Joyce

Go Bananas

It was a warm summer night and all the girl glow-worms in the field were busy glowing. The boy glow-worms were busy chasing them. The moon and the stars were glowing on everybody.

But Georgina wasn't glowing.

Georgina the glow-worm had

lost her glow.

Without my glow the other

glow-worms can't see me in the

dark, she thought sadly. How

will I ever make new friends?

She sat on her branch, and watched the dawn chase the night across the sky. The light was pink and opal. The clouds were like big sheep roaming through a blue field.

A teardrop slid slowly down
Georgina's cheek. In the pale dawn
sunlight, the tear shone like a star.

'Even my teardrops have a glow,'

said Georgina sadly.

The moon yawned sleepily and

went to bed.

'Good morning,' said a blackbird, landing in the hedge, the light from the sun brightening his beak. 'Why do you look so sad?'

'I've lost my glow,' said Georgina. 'Have you seen it?'

Oooh-er!

'What's a glow? Is it something to eat?' the blackbird asked.

I hope he doesn't eat glow-worms!

'No!' cried Georgina.

'You needn't shout,' said the blackbird. 'How am I expected to know? I don't glow. I fly.' And off he flew.

Georgina decided to search for her glow.

She set out across the field.

Dewdrops hung down from the grass,

sparkling in the light from the sun,

like tiny rainbows.

She came to a pond. The sun reflected in the water, like a huge orange beach ball.

'Good morning,' croaked a frog, sitting on a leaf and admiring himself in the surface of the pond. 'You look unhappy.' 'I've lost my glow,' said Georgina. 'I'm going to look for it.'

I'm so gorgeous.

Ugh!

'I've never had a glow,' said the frog.
'Not that I need one. I'm handsome enough without a glow. Just look at my reflection in the water. Don't you think I'm good-looking?'

'Very,' said Georgina, in case he ate her. 'Yes,' said the frog. 'I look at myself all day and I never get bored.'

Georgina sighed and went on searching. She saw a cockerel strutting on top of a farmhouse, its beautiful tail gleaming in the sunlight like a waterfall of feathers.

Ooh, handsome!

What a big-head!

She saw a pheasant
scurrying across the grass, like
a ball of fire shining in the sun.

She saw sunlight reflecting from the windows of the cottages in the village, and the screens of the cars in the lane.

She saw sunlight winking on
a weathervane and dazzling
from the top of a bus.

Georgina felt very sad. Everything in the world seemed to be shining, but Georgina still couldn't glow. So she crawled into a hole in a bank, to see if she was glowing in the dark. She wasn't. She sighed and closed her eyes.

A mole was busy digging a tunnel.

'You look miserable,' the mole said.

'I've lost my glow,' Georgina told

him. 'I don't like the dark. Nobody

can see me when it's dark.'

'I don't like light,' the mole replied.
'I think you can manage perfectly
well without it.'

'But I need to glow,' said Georgina.

'Do you mind doing it somewhere
else then,' said the mole.

I need a snooze.

Georgina climbed out of the hole.

Outside, it was twilight. She saw

a blaze of light in the field.

'What's that?' she gasped excitedly.

'It's a bonfire,' hissed a passing weasel.

'It's a glow,' Georgina said.

'Please yourself!' said the weasel

crossly and left.

The flames of the bonfire were

dancing in the water of the pond.

It was the most beautiful sight

Georgina had ever seen.

Crowds had gathered round to watch.

Some of them held torches, shining up

into the darkness.

Suddenly the sky filled with light.

Shooting stars raced into the darkness.

Fountains of colour danced and sparkled.

Catherine wheels whizzed and sizzled.

Rockets set off for the moon.

'What is it?' Georgina gasped.

'Fireworks,' snuffled a hedgehog.

'They're glowing,' Georgina sighed.

'They're noisy,' the hedgehog grumbled.

'But what are they for?' asked Georgina.

'It's a midsummer party, down
the farm,' said the hedgehog.
'To celebrate 21 June, the shortest
night of the year.'
And then he curled
up and rolled away.

I'm off.

Georgina went down
to the farm.

In the farmyard, she saw the farmer, going to milk the cows. He was carrying a lantern which glowed and shone on the straw in the barn. It was a warm, soft glow, and the cows went 'Moo' as if they enjoyed the light.

She climbed up a wall and looked through the window into the farmhouse. In the kitchen a big table was laid ready for the party. A fire was burning in the hearth, with flames jumping up the chimney and throwing shadows around the room.

How cosy!

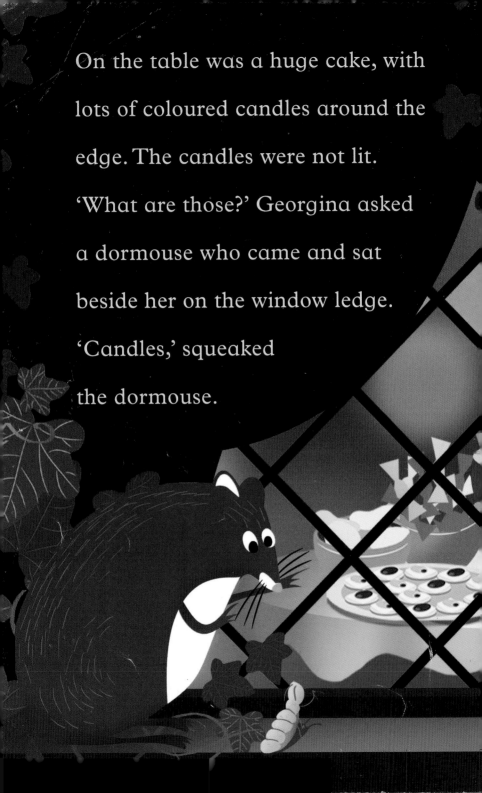

On the table was a huge cake, with lots of coloured candles around the edge. The candles were not lit.

'What are those?' Georgina asked a dormouse who came and sat beside her on the window ledge.

'Candles,' squeaked the dormouse.

'Do candles glow?' Georgina asked.

'Yes, but not until they're lit,' said the dormouse. 'They won't light them until the party begins.'

'I've never been to a party,' Georgina sighed.

'Noisy things,' said the dormouse.

'But lots of crumbs.'

Georgina went back to her hedge feeling very sad indeed. She climbed on to her branch and watched all the girl glow-worms glowing around her and all the boy glow-worms chasing them. Nobody noticed Georgina. She sat and stared at the moon. It was glowing. She stared at the stars.

Everything is glowing, except me.

They were glowing. Far away in the village she could see fairy-lights on the village green glowing. The bonfire was a big red glow in the field.

'I am the unhappiest glow-worm in the field,' Georgina said aloud.

There was a long silence.

Then suddenly, out of the dark,

somebody appeared.

It was a boy glow-worm.

He flew down out of the darkness and landed beside Georgina with a crash.

'Whoops!' he said. 'Sorry about that.

My name's Samuel. Who are you?'

'I'm Georgina,' she replied.

He was very handsome.

Georgina blushed.

'Do you want to come
to a party?' Samuel
asked her.

'Oh, yes please!' Georgina cried.

She had found a friend at last.

So Georgina and Samuel went to the party in the farmyard.

The blackbird and the frog sang lots
of songs, and the cockerel clapped
his claws.

The weasel danced with the hedgehog
while the dormouse danced with
the mole.

Inside the farm, the candles were lit on the cake, and the room glowed with candlelight.

A choir of crickets and nightingales sang in the trees, and in the bushes, all the glow-worms glowed.

Georgina and Samuel
danced together beneath the
light of the midsummer night moon.
'Oh, I do wish I had a glow like all
the other girls,' Georgina said sadly.
'I've been trying to glow all day.'

Aaah!

'But look!' cried Samuel. 'You are!'

Georgina looked round, and to her

surprise she saw the most wonderful

sight. A beautiful green glow.

'Is that me?' she gasped.

'Of course it's you,' Samuel laughed.

And it was!

What is a source of light?

A **source of light** is something that makes its own light — like the **sun**, **light bulbs**, **bonfires**, **fireworks**, **candles**, **stars** . . . and **glow-worms**, of course!

I'm a real, live source of light!

When she's fully grown, a female glow-worm can make her own light and glow for hours at a time.

Male glow-worms can't glow very well.

But we CAN fly!

The sun

The earth

The sun is the biggest and most important source of light.

The sun is the source of light for the earth. It makes daylight.

Remember, never look directly at the sun — it will hurt your eyes.

Because the sun is so bright, it's hard to see other sources of light when it's daytime.

I can't see Georgina's glow very well in the daytime.

What is darkness?

Darkness happens when there is no light. Because we need light to see things with, when it's dark, we can't see anything.

Night happens when our part of the earth moves away from the sun.

Most sources of light show up best at night-time. Can you find six sources of light in this picture?

I can't see anything in my underground home, because there are no sources of light. But I like the dark! I move about, dig and find my food by using my sense of smell, hearing, and touch.

Try this game with a friend!

Tell your friend to close their eyes, and place a small object in their hands. See if they can tell what it is by touching, hearing, or even smelling it.

Here are some ideas: egg, key, ball, hairclip, rubber, different kinds of fruit and vegetables.

Oy!

A pin cushion?

What is a reflection?

When light hits a shiny surface it bounces back, or is **reflected**. Shiny things like **mirrors**, **metal**, **glass** and **silver paper** all reflect light

Here are some shiny things that reflect light. Can you find them in the story?

The moon looks so bright because it reflects the light of the sun.

Did you know that birds called magpies like to collect shiny objects that reflect light? They use them to make their nests look nice and attract mates!

Make your own glittery disco ball!

What you'll need:

1 small round potato

1 piece of string about 30cm long

3 large pieces of tinfoil

glue

1 torch

1 grown-up to help!

Now here's the fun part. Have a hunt around the house for all the glittery things you can find! Anything that reflects light really well, like silvery sweet wrappers, milk-bottle tops, tinsel and sequins.

1 First take your potato and ask a grown-up to tie the string around it like a parcel.

2 To make your disco ball, first take one piece of tinfoil and wrap it around your potato like this.

3 Then take the next piece of tinfoil and wrap it over the top of the first piece. Scrunch the foil gently and make a round ball shape.

4 Wrap the final piece of tinfoil around your ball. Scrunch it gently. All the folds and crinkles in the foil will reflect the light and make your disco ball sparkle like the sun!

Get scrunching!

Keep the string poking out like this.

5 Now, use glue to stick your glittery bits and bobs to your disco ball.

6 Ask a grown-up to help you hang it up where everyone can see it.

Now it's party time! Wait till it gets dark (or just shut your curtains), put on your favourite music, and shine a torch on your amazing glitter ball!

If you spin it around, it'll look even groovier!

Groovy move!

Rainbows

Have you ever seen a rainbow? Next time it's sunny and rainy at the same time, have a look outside. Rainbows are made when raindrops reflect the sun's light. In fairy tales, if you find the end of the rainbow, you'll discover a pot of shiny gold!

We've found the end of the rainbow!

You can make your very own rainbow!

Ask an adult to place a glass of water on a window-sill, on a bright, sunny day.

Ask them to place the glass so that the edge just hangs over the edge of the sill (be careful it doesn't fall off!). A rainbow should form on the floor!